I am My Grandpa's Enkelin

Walter Wangerin, Jr.

ILLUSTRATED BY Don Tate

PARACLETE PRESS
BREWSTER, MA

For Theron,
Merciful hunter and my grandson
WW

To the students, teachers, parents, and administrators of
Strickland Christian School, Austin, Texas
DT

I am My Grandpa's Enkelin

2007   First Printing

Text copyright 2007 by Walter Wangerin, Jr.
Illustrations copyright 2007 by Donald Tate

ISBN 978-1-55725-468-9

Library of Congress Cataloging-in-Publication Data
Wangerin, Walter.
I am my grandpa's Enkelin / by Walter Wangerin, Jr. ; illustrated by Don Tate.
p. cm.
Summary: The granddaughter of a German-American farmer tells of her experiences
with him on the farm and the many things he taught her about life.
ISBN 978-1-55725-468-9
[1. Grandfathers--Fiction. 2. Farm life—Fiction. 3. German Americans—Fiction.]
I. Tate, Don, ill. II. Title.
PZ7.W1814Iae 2007
[Fic]—dc22   2007031286

All rights reserved. No portion of this book may be reproduced, stored in an electronic
retrieval system, or transmitted in any form or by any means—electronic, mechanical,
photocopy, recording, or any other—except for brief quotations in printed reviews,
without the prior permission of the publisher.

Published by Paraclete Press • Brewster, Massachusetts • www.paracletepress.com

10 9 8 7 6 5 4 3 2 1

Printed in Singapore

Spring

When I was a little girl
My grandpa plowed behind two horses.
He called the black horse Prince:
"Get up, Prince!" he'd say. "Get up—"
And the earth was turned by the plow blade, black.
Whenever he saw me running across the field,
Old honey buckets hanging from my hands,
Grandpa said to the dappled horse,
"Whoa, Silver, whoa!
Here comes that pretty *Enkelin* with my lunch."

In one bucket, bread and sausages;
In the other, grandpa's coffee, hot and black—
And a little sip for me.

Sometimes when he finished eating
Grandpa would stretch out
In the shade of a maple tree,
Then stick a toothpick in his mouth,
And point it at the sky,
And tell me tales of chickens and snails
And foxes who crept through the night.

After lunch,
When he began to plow again,
With the reins across his shoulders,
And when I turned to carry the buckets home,
The day was so quiet, so quiet the day,
That I could hear
The horses snort,
And the drag of the plow,
And grandpa singing in German:
"Du, du, liegst mir im Herzen—"
Nodding and calling,
"Mein Enkelin is going away."

Before supper it was my job
To lead the big horses down to the pond
To let them drink the water
Where geese and the ducks
Teach their hatchlings how to swim.
But the closer the horses came to the water,
The harder they blew and the faster they trotted,
And I, so short between their shoulders,
Hurried, hurried to keep up:
Watch out!
Watch out for hooves as big as my head!
Then stop! Stop!
Before they stop and I fly into the pond!

On Saturday nights we all ate the popcorn
Grandpa had planted and picked
And grandma had shucked and shelled.
We played cards in the parlor—
Then prayed our prayers while the old dog barked
And one cow lowed
And a dreaming chicken clucked her fears
And the fox crept to the coop,
Making no sound at all.

Summer

When I was a little girl
And grandpa's corn grew west of the house
("Knee-high by the Fourth of July,"
And then it tassled taller than I!),

Grandma kept a criss-cross garden
In the yard to the east.
Peas were the first to ripen.
We popped them from their pods
And dropped them, bump and tumble,
    in the pot.

Radishes, lettuces, spinach, and kale,
Pole beans, peonies, cucumbers, dill,
Roses, petunias, snapdragons, dahlias,
Tomatoes and berries both red and black—
The vegetables we cooked and canned,
The fruits we turned into jellies and jams,
And the house was filled with grandma's flowers,
Sunlight on the stormiest day.

My jobs:
I dropped slops in the pigpen.
I scattered feed for the chickens.
I gathered their eggs,
    still warm to my hands—
But the worst, let me tell you:
The worst job on grandpa's farm
Was cleaning out the chicken coop
Of chicken poop!

In July, behind black Prince and dappled Silver,
Grandpa mowed the fields of green alfalfa.
He raked the mown alfalfa into windrows,
Long and winding, moist and as dark as secrets.
Weeks later, when it had dried to brown,
Still lying on the ground,
The alfalfa had turned to hay,
Food for the cows in the winter.
So grandpa and my uncle Hans
Drove Prince and Silver back to the fields
Pulling a wagon wide and flat.
The horses drew the wagon along the rows
While uncle Hans gathered hay on a fork
And tossed the bundle up to grandpa,
Who caught that bundle on another fork
And laid it on the wagon,
Bundles and bundles,
Building the hay-pile higher and higher,
Weaving it tight so it wouldn't fall,
Climbing the hay-pile as it grew,
Climbing so high
That when the horses pulled the wagon toward the barn
My grandpa could look straight across,
Straight into my bedroom window!
"Du, du liegst mir im Herzen,"
My grandpa sang as he passed me by,
Bowing and tipping the brim of his hat:
"Du, du liegst mir im Sinn!"

One August day,
Hot and humid and long and humdrum,
I sneaked between the cornrows with a book to read.
But soon, in the buzzing heat, I fell asleep.
I dreamed that the foxes were licking my face
With tongues as sharp as knives.
I dreamed the birds were fluttering above me,
Whispering, *The girl is lost! The girl is lost!*
And who can find her now?
Suddenly I woke up.
No, it wasn't foxes' tongues;
It was the long leaves of the cornstalks!
No, it wasn't whispering birds,
But a breeze in the leaves around me.
All around me!
Which way was out?
I got up and ran down one row.
I cut through the stalks
And ran down another;
But I couldn't find the way out anywhere!
"Grandpa!" I yelled.
"Grandpa!" I wailed:
"This little girl is lost, and who can find me now?"
Far, far away I heard a voice call: *"Enkelin!"*

10

But it was so far away
That it seemed to come from everywhere,
Everywhere, anywhere, nowhere at all!
"Enkelin!"
It was my grandpa.
I heard his voice say, "Do not run!
Do not move.
The field is too huge!
But sing the song with me
And shake a cornstalk to the beat,
And I will hear you where you are."
Grandpa started the song,
And I shouted as loud as I could:
"DU! DU! LIEGST MIR IM HERZEN!
DU! DU LIEGST MIR IM SINN!"
Grandpa sang another line:
"Du, du machst mir viel schmerzen—"
By then his voice was just two rows away,
So I started to cry,
And he crashed through the tall corn
And picked me up
And carried me, and whispered in my ear,
"Stille, stille."

That night,
Even before we finished our supper
Of a fine fat duck,
Roasted to a crunchy brown,
Grandpa bowed his head and prayed:
"Lord, I will not always be nearby
To find *mein Enkelin* when she is lost.
Stay with her.
Be to her the hen
That gathers her chicks to her bosom at night."
Then he sighed.

After supper he popped a toothpick into his mouth,
And strolled outside to stand in the mown alfalfa field.
I watched my grandpa,
Standing black against the starry sky.
A bent-backed man, a mighty shadow,
That toothpick sticking out
Like a tiny sword of glory
And protection.

And sometimes before the planting
I would see this too:
Grandpa, dark in the twilight,
Would kneel down
And gather soil in his hand
And hold it to his nose
To judge if the earth was ready for seed.
My grandpa knew the earth right well,
And the night,
And the darkness—
And me, too.

14

Autumn

When I was a little girl,
The cows walked narrow paths
From the barnyard to the harvested fields
Where grandpa let them graze
On fallen ears and grain.

Mornings, they walked out on their own.
Evenings, I went with the dog to drive them home again;
Not very hard work.
Their milk bags were full.
They wanted to come.

But when we passed the yard
Where grandpa kept the bull,
I went by at a fast skip.
That bull would charge at people.
Once I saw my uncle Hans take off
And sail right over the barbed-wire fence,
The bull's horns right behind him!

When October came
And the wind tore leaves from the trees,
We gathered potatoes and squashes,
Pears and nuts and gourds and pumpkins,
Apples for cider, apples for sauce,
Apples whole to eat in winter;
We gathered them in bushels and bags
And stored them in the rootcellar,
All rich with smells
Sweet and tingling and full of earth,
And a cool stroke to the skin.

We kept a lantern in that cellar,
Ever full of kerosene,
Even in the spring and summer,
Because this is where we would hide
When the sky turned yellow-green
And the wind dead-still
And the dog's hair rose all down his spine—
Signs that a tornado might drop down from heaven
And sweep the house away.

During one of the coldest days in
    November
Neighbors came with food
And boards for trestle tables
And enormous iron pots
And wooden spoons as long as my leg
For rendering the fat of the hogs
That grandpa was butchering that day.
One perfect knock in the head
And the hog was dead.

Two strong men dipped the body
In a barrel of boiling water
To make the bristles soft enough
To scrape them from the skin.
Oh, we worked hard the daylong,
Stringing the hogs up by their hind hooves
In the doorway of a shed,
cleaning the guts out,
Saving the good parts,
Intestines to pack sausages,
The heart, the kidneys and liver
(Don't you just love the kidneys and liver?).

We cooled lard for frying and baking,
Roasted cracklings of the flesh,
Ground meat for stuffing sausages,
Cut hams and chops
And fatback for bacon.
We hung these cuts in our little smokehouse
Which soon was cloudy with hickory smoke
To preserve our meat,
To make it tasty and safe
For eating in the winter—
All these good things
    we shared with our neighbors.

Afterward everyone
Ate outside at one long, long trestle table,
Chicken and beans and potato salad
And cakes and pies
    and laughter and happiness.
And there at the head of the table
My grandpa grinned
And flipped a toothpick round his mouth.
These were the people we saw in church
On Sunday mornings,
The day we did no work at all
(Except to milk the cows).

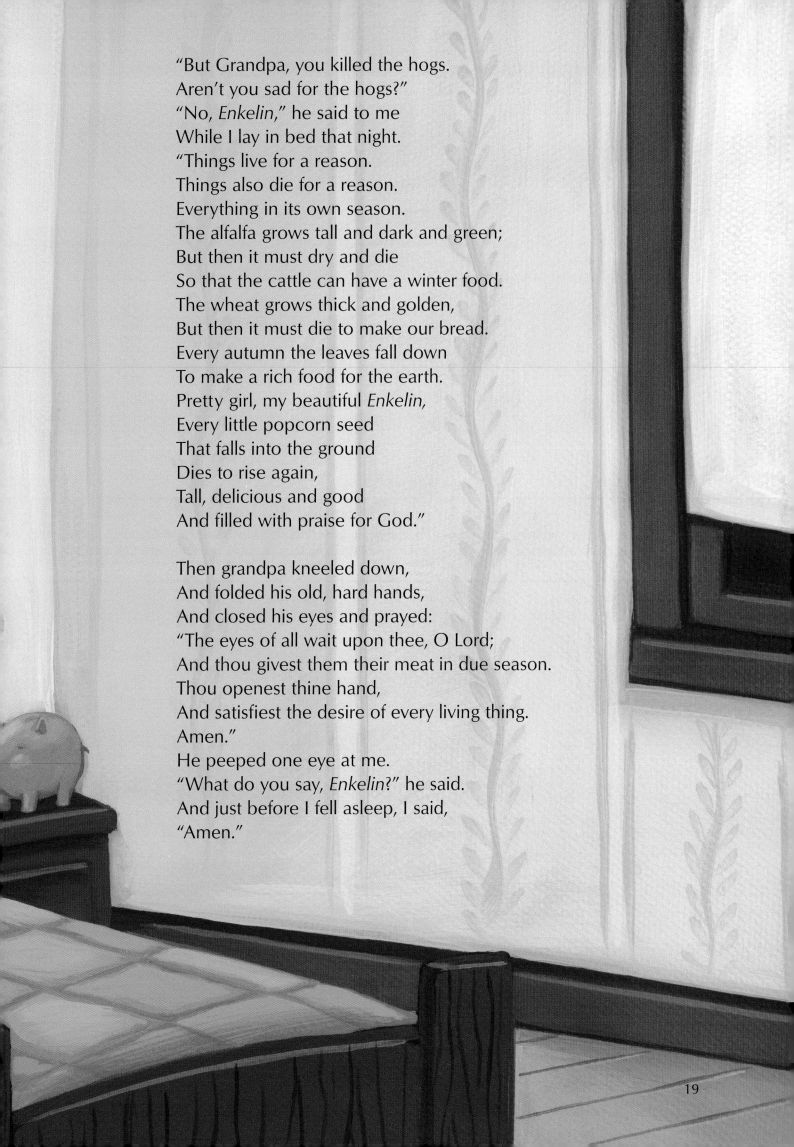

"But Grandpa, you killed the hogs.
Aren't you sad for the hogs?"
"No, *Enkelin*," he said to me
While I lay in bed that night.
"Things live for a reason.
Things also die for a reason.
Everything in its own season.
The alfalfa grows tall and dark and green;
But then it must dry and die
So that the cattle can have a winter food.
The wheat grows thick and golden,
But then it must die to make our bread.
Every autumn the leaves fall down
To make a rich food for the earth.
Pretty girl, my beautiful *Enkelin*,
Every little popcorn seed
That falls into the ground
Dies to rise again,
Tall, delicious and good
And filled with praise for God."

Then grandpa kneeled down,
And folded his old, hard hands,
And closed his eyes and prayed:
"The eyes of all wait upon thee, O Lord;
And thou givest them their meat in due season.
Thou openest thine hand,
And satisfiest the desire of every living thing.
Amen."
He peeped one eye at me.
"What do you say, *Enkelin*?" he said.
And just before I fell asleep, I said,
"Amen."

Winter

When I was a little girl,
There was no bathroom in grandpa's farmhouse.
Even on the coldest days
We went to sit in the two-hole outhouse
On the far side of the kitchen yard, freezing our behinders.

Neither did the house have a furnace.
Grandpa kept a coal stove in the dining room
And grandma used a wood stove in the kitchen.
She lit her fires with corncobs
And with fire heated water in a tank attached to the stove
And baked her cakes with fire.

Early, early in the mornings
When I heard grandpa lighting the coal stove below,
I woke with frost on the blanket beneath my nose.
I dressed under the covers.
Then grandpa and I went outside together
Into the zero cold, into the perfect wintry darkness.
Time to milk the cows.
The barn was warmed by the cows inside.
Grandpa had a one-legged stool
Which he sat on when he reached to wash
The cow's milk-bag and then her teats.
Next he squeezed those teats between his fingers, swiftly,
Laying his cheek against her warm flank,
Squirting needle-shots of milk
Into the pail between his ankles.
Sometimes he aimed a squirt at the barn cats
Who caught the mice and rats
And loved milk straight from the cow.
When his pails grew full, I carried them away.
I poured the foaming milk into large cans,
Cans too big for me to carry. So grandpa hefted them
And heaved them outside toward the milk house,
Where there was a flow-well, even in the winter.

21

Our boots squeaked on the crusted snow.
The dawn caused a dim-dark grey
Above the trees past the garden side of the house.
Our breath blew white clouds into the still air.

"Listen, *Enkelin*, what do you hear?"
"Nothing," I said. "I don't hear anything."
"But I hear something."
Grandpa set the milk can down
And stooped to lean on it.
"I hear the voice of God.
Sometimes silence is how God talks the loudest."
"What is God saying?"
"Well, God is saying,
'How beautiful is the night;
How beautiful is the deep;
How beautiful my white blanket
That covers the earth in sleep.'
God is saying,
'Grandpa, old man, don't you think so too?'"
"Do you?" I said. "Do you think so too?"
"Oh, yes, yes. Always.
All the things that God has made
Are beautiful,
Even the sleep at the end."

"Grandpa?"
"What."
"What does that song mean, the song we sing?"
My grandpa sighed
And sat down on the lid of the milk can
And lifted me to his knee.
"Sing it," he whispered. "But slowly, slowly."
I sang, *"Du, du liegst mir im Herzen—"*
"You, you," my grandpa said, "abide in my heart."
"Du, du liegst mir im Sinn—"
"And you, *mein Enkelin*, are always on my mind."
"Yes, and there was another line, grandpa.
When you came to find me in the corn
You sang about—
I think—
Was the word *Schmerzen*?"
"Ach, but the meaning of that word you must learn
When your heart is ready to learn it.
Get up. Let's carry this milk inside
Before it freezes."

The Last Spring

When I was still a little girl—
(Big in my body, going to college
Two hundred miles away from the farm,
But still a little girl inside my heart)—
I lost my grandpa in the spring.

He had not finished planting the corn seeds.
Grandma said he lay down under the maple tree
Where once he told me tales.
She brought his lunch in honey buckets.
He saw her arrive beside him.
He smiled.
He breathed three quick breaths,
And then he died.

"Please come," my grandma said on the telephone.
"You must be here for his funeral."

I was so sad.
My baby-heart hurt as if it were a burning stove
Or a little fox chewing inside my chest.

I took a bus from school back to the farm.
Grandpa, I thought, you were not supposed to die.
You were supposed to be near me always,
To find your *Enkelin* whenever she got lost.
But I felt lost right then,
Sitting on the bus,
Looking out the window
At all the farmers in their fields,
On tractors,
Planting corn seeds in the ground.

Uncle Hans, who had grey hair now,
Drove me from the bus station
Into the barnyard.
Grandma came on the porch to meet me;
And I, when I felt her arms around me,
I started to cry.
"*Stille, stille*," my little old grandma
Whispered in my ears.
I looked around while she held me.

While I was crying, I looked around,
My eyesight blurry with salty water.
It seemed to me that all the animals were standing still.
The chickens were sad. The cows were sad.
The ducks and ducklings, the geese and the goslings
Waddled close and bent their necks.
The old dog hung his head with sorrow.
But Prince and Silver, where were they?
Grandma said, "They didn't last, my child.
They must have known that something was coming to pass.
Honey, grandpa's horses lay down in the winter
And let the snowfall cover them."

Grandma stood back and took my hands.
"Come, child," she said.
"Let's go say goodbye to your grandpa
Where he lies in the funeral home."

And there, crowded inside, were all the people
Who had shared the farmwork with grandpa,
All who helped when he butchered the hogs,
All who sat in church around us every Sunday,
Crowded in a bright room
With my grandpa at the end of it,
Lying in a casket.

Even among these people I still felt lost,
As if they were rows and rows of murmuring cornstalks.

Du, du, I heard in my heart:
Liegst mir im Herzen.
Du, du liegst mir im Sinn—
And suddenly I remembered the whole next line,
As if grandpa had just sung it in my soul:
Du, du machst mir viel Schmerzen—
And I knew his language too,
And I understood what these words meant:
You, you cause me such pain!
Yes, grandpa—you cause me pain
As I walk through this crowd
To look at your last, lonely lying place.

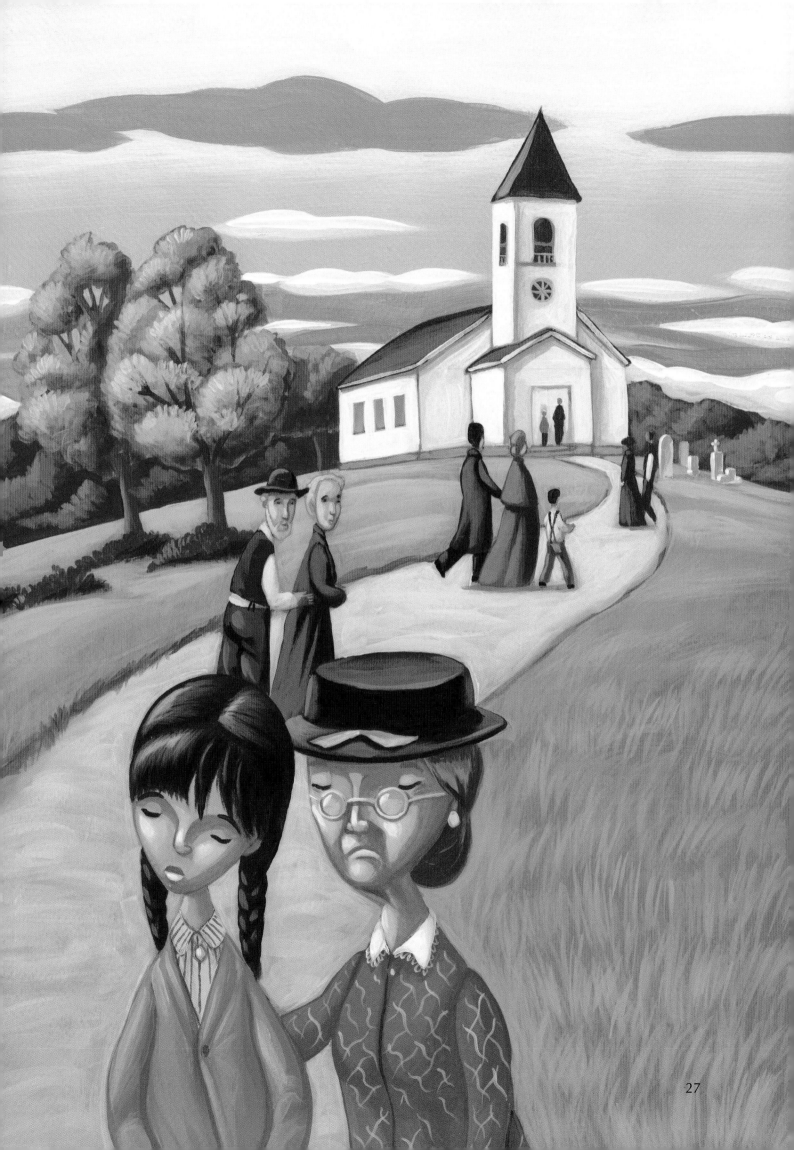

No,
But it was grandpa who sang that line,
About *me*.
Had I caused him pain in his heart?
Could it be the sweet pain of love
That his *Enkelin* had caused him?

Then,
Standing by the casket,
Finally,
I looked down.
I looked at the face of my grandpa,
And what I saw there tickled me.

I put my hand to my mouth.
Is it okay to laugh in a funeral home?
I couldn't help it.
I giggled.
I started to laugh.
All of grandpa's friends—
They, too, were tittering and giggling.
So then I let myself laugh hard and happily,
Even till my sides ached from the
    laughing—

Because there,
Sticking out of the corner of his mouth,
Was that brave toothpick—
"Grandma!" I cried. "Did you—?"
She nodded.
And look:
My grandpa was grinning!

The First Spring of All

I am a big girl now.

And now I know
That when I was still a little girl,
I had gotten it all wrong.

In fact grandpa had finished planting
All his seeds!
Because, in that spring,
He had planted
His last and his best seed of all.
He had stood in the spring field before plowing,
In the twilight,
A brave black shadow
Against the starlight;
He had held the soil up to his nose
To judge whether it was ready
For one tough seed.

It was ready.
The earth was ready for this,
His most important planting.
It was himself.
He was the seed.

And one day, years from now,
But in a day exactly right,
Grandpa will rise
Higher than the cornstalks,
Higher than the haystack,
Higher than the farmhouse
And the barn
And the smoke that goes up from our little
    smokehouse.
Grandpa will rise with his little sword of glory,
Exactly like the man of heaven.

Even now, while waiting,
Grandpa peeps one eye at me,
His grown-up girl.
What do you say, Enkelin? grandpa whispers.
And I know exactly what to say.
I say, "Amen."
And I say it again:
"Amen."